4 Adventure Stories

SCHOLASTIC INC. Cartwheel B·O·O·K·S®

New York Toronto London Auckland Sydney
Mexico City New Delhi Hong Kong Buenos Aires

Batman®: *Time Thaw* (0-439-47096-X)
Copyright © 2003 by DC Comics.

Batman®: *The Copycat Crime* (0-439-47097-8)
Copyright © 2003 by DC Comics.

Batman®: *The Mad Hatter* (0-439-47098-6)
Copyright © 2004 by DC Comics.

Batman®: *The Purr-fect Crime* (0-439-47100-1)
Copyright © 2004 by DC Comics.

Copyright © 2005 by DC Comics.
Batman and all related characters and elements are trademarks of and © DC Comics.
All rights reserved. Published by Scholastic Inc.
SCHOLASTIC, CARTWHEEL BOOKS, and associated logos
are trademarks and/or registered trademarks of Scholastic Inc.

ISBN 0-439-76312-6

12 11 10 9 8 7 6 5 4 3 2 1   5 6 7 8 9 10/0
Printed in the U.S.A. 56 • This compilation edition first printing, June 2005

Written by **Jesse Leon McCann**

Illustrated by **John Byrne**

Batman created by Bob Kane

CHAPTER ONE

CREATURE FEATURE

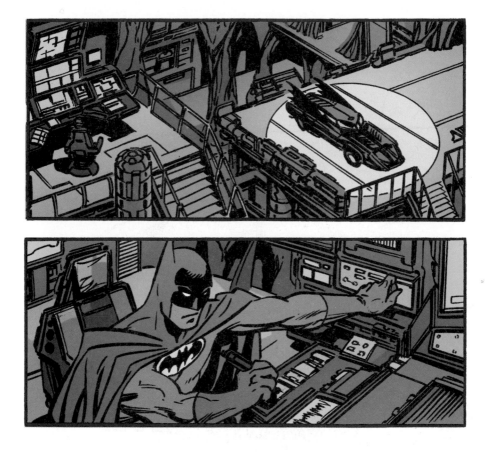

Bruce Wayne was one of the richest men in Gotham City. He lived in Wayne Manor, above a secret cave — the Batcave!

That's because Bruce was also Batman!

Every evening Batman carefully checked his crime-fighting tools and equipment. Tonight he was almost ready to go out on patrol.

A STRANGE *FOG* HAD COVERED *GOTHAM CITY.*

It was a cold night in Gotham City. Police
detectives Harvey Bullock and Renee
Montoya shivered inside their squad car.

They were not happy. A strange fog had
covered Gotham the last three nights. The
fog was very cold and thick. And every cop
had to work long hours.

THOOM!

Montoya's eyes grew wide. "What was that?"

THOOM! THOOM! The ground shook.

"Good question!" Bullock said. He quickly wiped the window with a rag.

They looked out into the soupy fog. What they saw was chilling. Very big creatures were coming at them from the mist!

THOOM! THOOM! THOOM!

And then . . . *CRUNCH!*

One huge beast stepped on the front of their car. It crushed the hood flat.

"Holy cow!" Bullock jumped from the car. "Get out, Montoya! That thing isn't going around us!"

Montoya rolled out onto the cold street. She looked back to see the creature wreck their car . . . *CRUNCH! CRUNCH!* Then it went on down the road.

The two detectives rubbed their eyes.

They watched the beasts disappear into the fog.

The enormous creatures looked like mastodons, giant sloths, and woolly mammoths! But those prehistoric creatures had been extinct for thousands of years—since the Ice Age!

CHAPTER TWO

FOG FACTORY

As the mist rolled in for a third night, Batman the Dark Knight was in his Batplane. He was flying over the ocean.

Batman knew something was wrong. He had been checking the weather satellite all day. It was always the same: Clear. But this fog was not natural!

The fog was coming from the east. That part of the ocean was dotted with small islands. Maybe these islands held the answer to the fog.

Sure enough, on one rocky island, he spotted a huge factory. Several smokestacks poured out big clouds of thick, cold, man-made fog.

The only place to land was the factory's roof. Batman turned on the landing gear and set the plane down.

He stepped outside the plane. Frost crunched under his boots. The smokestacks were covered with four inches of ice!

Just then Batman's radio buzzed. Commissioner Gordon was calling him.

"Batman, it's the craziest thing," Commissioner Gordon said. "We've been

invaded—by a pack of prehistoric animals.

We need you!"

"I'll be there in fifteen minutes."

Batman turned back to the Batplane.

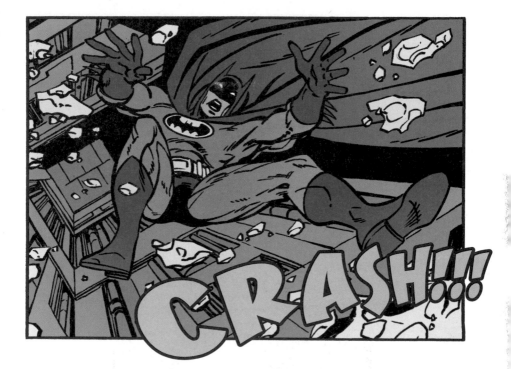

The mystery of the fog-making factory

would have to wait!

But he didn't reach the Batplane.

Suddenly, a trap door in the roof opened

under him and he was falling! *WHOMP!*

He landed on a cold concrete floor.

"Ah, Batman. I thought it was you. Welcome!"

Batman knew that voice.

It was Mr. Freeze!

CHAPTER THREE

FAREWELL, BATMAN!

Batman got to his feet. "What's this about, Mr. Freeze?" he asked.

Mr. Freeze was on a platform twenty feet above the ground. He looked down meanly at the Dark Knight.

"Revenge, my old enemy... for what has been done to my life!"

Mr. Freeze was once a scientist named Dr. Victor Fries. He did experiments in super-cold temperatures. But a laboratory accident had changed Fries. He now needed to live in a special freezing cold suit.

Dr. Fries became Mr. Freeze! He turned to crime to pay for his plans to turn Gotham City into an icy, frozen land.

"I'm sure you've heard about the strange creatures in your foggy city," Freeze said. He pushed a button on a panel. The lights inside the factory went on.

"I was lucky to find my prehistoric friends during a recent dig in Siberia," Freeze said with a laugh.

Batman looked around. He knew he

would have to fight soon—possibly for his life. So he used this time to listen and prepare.

"I was digging for a special diamond, the Sol Stone," Freeze went on. "It's the last piece I need for my laser-pulse ice cannon."

Freeze pushed another button. Beneath him, the floor opened. A hovercraft rose to ground level. On it was a huge, dangerous looking cannon.

"One blast and Gotham City will freeze forever," Freeze said. He stepped onto the hovercraft. "However, I didn't find the Sol Stone—just creatures frozen for thousands of years. Now they and my freezing fog will keep the police busy while I finally get my Sol Stone!"

ON THE *HOVERCRAFT* WAS A *DANGEROUS LOOKING* CANNON!

"By stealing it!" Batman said.

"An excellent guess, Batman," the cold criminal laughed. "How lucky for me it's on display at the Gotham Museum."

Mr. Freeze flipped a switch. A part of the wall to the outside opened. Batman ran after the hovercraft.

Mr. Freeze flipped another switch. Another part of the wall opened. Out leaped two giant, snarling creatures.

Saber-toothed tigers!

"Farewell, Batman!" Freeze steered the craft outside. The wall began to close behind him. "Play nicely with my pets!"

Now Batman was alone with the circling tigers. He stayed still. The tigers would leap at the slightest move.

Batman reached slowly for his utility belt.

That was all it took.

GROWL!

A tiger roared and leaped. It hit Batman hard, knocking him backward!

Batman back-flipped away from the tiger's slashing claws. With his last flip, he leaped over the growling beast.

The second cat was waiting. Batman was forced to kick it in the head. The tiger was briefly stunned. Then Batman ran as fast as he could toward Mr. Freeze's platform.

But the tigers were faster. One of them slammed him down from behind. Batman rolled onto his back as the cat slashed at him with razor-sharp claws.

Would that moment be the end of the Dark Knight?

CHAPTER FOUR

A QUIET MIST

In one quick move, Batman grabbed a mask and gas capsule from his utility belt. He covered his mouth and nose with the mask. Then he threw the capsule to the floor. A thick mist rose from the capsule.

THE KNOCKOUT GAS HAD WORKED!

The two giant cats keeled over and passed out. The knockout gas had worked!

The sleeping tigers were now as harmless as kittens. Batman climbed to the roof. Mr. Freeze was way ahead of him—and Batman needed to get to the Batplane as soon as possible!

Batman skidded to a stop on the icy roof. He saw that Mr. Freeze had done one last thing before escaping.

The Batplane's engines were frozen solid!

CHAPTER FIVE

MAMMOTH IN THE MUSEUM

Mr. Freeze had planned perfectly. No one paid attention as he froze the Gotham City Museum's alarm system. Then he flew his hovercraft through the big doors of the museum's loading dock.

Inside, Freeze found the Sol Stone. He had to be careful. If he set off a different special alarm, a cage would drop over the display case. And that would trap him.

Luckily, a quick blast from his freeze gun silenced the alarm. The Sol Stone was his!

Mr. Freeze smashed the glass display and grabbed the big diamond. With this, his cannon's laser would be much more powerful. Soon, Gotham City would be in ice forever!

The Sol Stone was beautiful, as delicate as a snowflake. He held it up to admire it. And then...

FWHAAP!

A Batarang hit Freeze's wrist! The Sol Stone went flying. It was snatched from the air by a gloved hand.

The villain was shocked to see Batman.
The Dark Knight was riding one of Freeze's
own woolly mammoths!

"What?" Freeze raged. "How?"

BATMAN HAD **WHISKED** TOWARD GOTHAM CITY IN HIS **BATGLIDER**.

Batman almost smiled. There was no need to tell the villain the truth. When he saw the Batplane had been frozen, Batman had thought of another way to leave the island!

Climbing into the cockpit, the Dark Knight strapped on his Batglider. Then he pulled the airplane's ejector-seat lever. With a blast, he was shot straight up, high into the night sky!

His Batglider wings opened. As the wind filled them, he whisked toward Gotham City. During his flight, he called his trusted aide, Alfred.

"Prepare a barrel of sleeping gas," Batman ordered.

When he landed, Batman quickly found a fire truck. He then attached a hose to the knockout gas. Driving around town, Batman used the sleeping gas on all the giant prehistoric animals. Before long, they were snoozing peacefully in the streets.

He found the last mammoth outside the Gotham Museum…but his knockout gas was gone! Luckily, as millionaire Bruce Wayne, Batman had ridden elephants many times on safari in India. Batman rode the huge beast into the museum. And that's when he met up again with Mr. Freeze.

But Mr. Freeze didn't even wait for Batman to answer. He raised his freeze gun and growled, "You've been so worried about my big freeze gun, you've forgotten about this little one!"

THE DARK KNIGHT RODE THE *HUGE BEAST* INTO THE *MUSEUM.*

CHAPTER SIX

A FREEZING FIGHT

Mr. Freeze shot Batman with a blast from his freeze gun. Batman was trapped from the shoulders down in solid ice.

BATMAN FELL TO THE FLOOR...FROZEN!

He fell to the floor at the mammoth's feet.

The Sol Stone dropped to the ground. Mr. Freeze snatched it up and returned to his ice cannon. "Once the gem is in place, I will be unstoppable!" he shouted.

Batman had to act quickly. He rolled his ice-covered body into the mammoth's foot. The creature lifted its foot and then stepped on him, cracking open the ice! Before the beast's foot could hurt him, Batman quickly rolled out from under it.

Mr. Freeze was fitting the diamond into his cannon. Batman jumped across the room, tackling the villain. The startled Mr. Freeze struggled as Batman quickly tied him with his Batrope. Batman plucked the Sol Stone from the ice cannon. Freeze's plot was over!

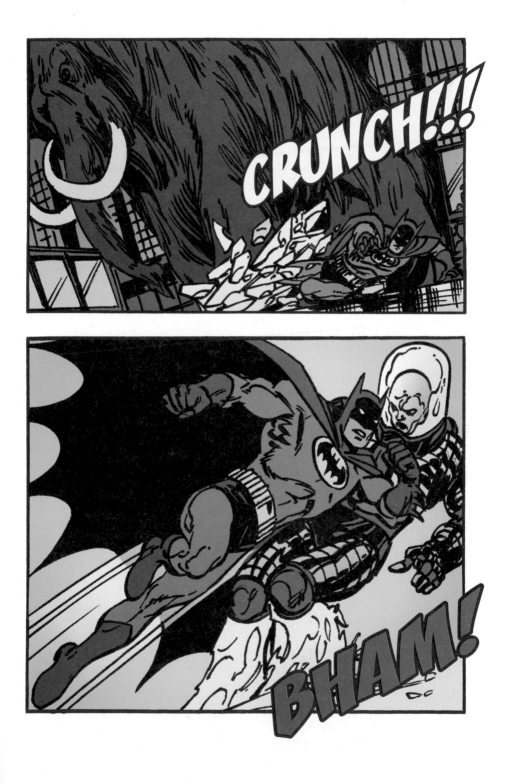

Later, Batman—now dressed as Bruce Wayne—and Alfred sat by a crackling fire in the parlor of Wayne Manor. They watched the fog outside the windows slowly disappear.

Batman had made sure Mr. Freeze was safely with the police. The deadly ice cannon was in pieces. Then Batman had returned to the island and destroyed Freeze's fog factory.

"I heard the prehistoric creatures have found a new home in the Gotham Zoo," Alfred said. He poured more hot tea. "A fine and chilly night's work, Master Bruce."

"Yes, Alfred," Bruce smiled. "But nothing warms me more than knowing Gotham City is safe."

THE COPYCAT CRIME

Written by **Devin Grayson**
Illustrated by **John Byrne**

Batman created by Bob Kane

CHAPTER ONE

MISSING PERSON

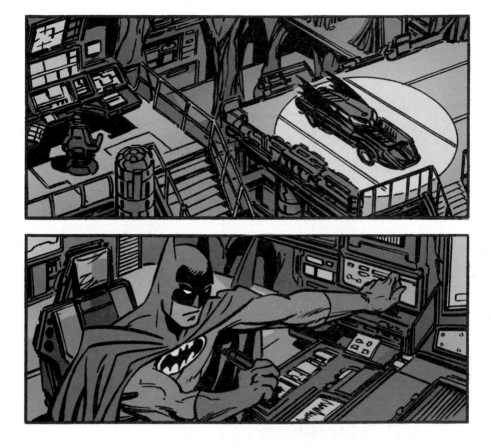

Bruce Wayne was one of the richest men in Gotham City. He lived in Wayne Manor, above a secret cave — the Batcave!

That's because Bruce was also Batman!

Every evening Batman carefully checked his crime-fighting tools and equipment. Tonight he was almost ready to go out on patrol.

Meanwhile, young Brian Fletcher was checking his math homework. Brian lived on the other side of Gotham City.

He looked at his watch. It was dinner-time. But Brian's mother wasn't home yet. She was a detective. Many nights she came home late.

Brian went to the refrigerator. He took out the peanut butter, the jelly, and the bread. He made two sandwiches. Brian poured himself a glass of milk. Then he sat down to dinner alone.

Two hours later, Detective Fletcher walked into her house.

"Brian!" she called.

But Brian didn't answer.

Detective Fletcher went into the kitchen. She saw a plate with crumbs and an empty

glass of milk from Brian's dinner.

"Brian!" she called again.

Still, no answer. Detective Fletcher ran into Brian's room. On his bed, she found a note. It read: What is the tallest building in Gotham City?

"A ransom note in the form of a riddle!" cried Detective Fletcher. "That could only mean...the Riddler!"

Detective Fletcher called her captain. "The Riddler has kidnapped Brian!" she cried. "I found a riddle on Brian's bed. It said: What is the tallest building in Gotham City?"

"The tallest building in Gotham City is the Wayne Enterprises building," said the captain. "I'll get some squad cars over there right away. Meet me there!"

CHAPTER TWO

RIDDLE ME THIS

Six squad cars surrounded the Wayne Enterprises building. All night long, the police officers searched the building. But Brian was nowhere to be found.

After twenty-two hours, Brian was still missing. Detective Fletcher met with Commissioner Gordon.

"Please find my boy," she begged.

"We're doing everything we can," said the commissioner.

A third voice added, "And we'll do more." Detective Fletcher jumped at the sound. She thought that she and the commissioner were alone.

Then someone stepped out from the shadows of the alley. It was crime fighter Batman.

"We need your help, Batman," said Detective Fletcher. "I found this note on my son's bed. We've searched every inch of the Wayne Enterprises building, but we haven't found him."

Batman looked at the note. "This looks like the work of the Riddler."

"That's what we thought," said the

commissioner. "But the Riddler was in jail when it happened."

CHAPTER THREE

A DOUBTFUL DUO

"We've asked the Riddler to help us find Brian," the commissioner said to Batman.

The commissioner led Batman and Detective Fletcher to a police car. The sly Riddler was inside. "Hello, Batman," the villain grinned. "Why is seeing you today like taking a vacation?"

"I don't know," said Batman. "But what do you know about Brian Fletcher?" He held up the riddle about the tallest building.

The Riddler laughed. "Is that the riddle you need me to help you solve?" he asked.

"It's the only clue we have," said the commissioner. "The answer is the Wayne Enterprises building. But we didn't find the boy there."

"You won't solve this if you think like a grown-up," said the Riddler.

"What do you mean?" Batman asked.

"The kid wasn't kidnapped," said the Riddler. "I bet he ran away from home. He's the one who wrote that riddle."

"Do you know where we can find him?" asked Detective Fletcher.

"No," said the Riddler. "But I'd be
happy to look!"

He kicked out the screen between
the front and backseats. The screen hit
the driver in the head. The driver
slumped over.

Batman tried to stop the Riddler.

But the Riddler was too fast. He climbed

into the driver's seat. Then he sped off,

shouting, "Why is seeing you today like

going on vacation? Because it means I can

get away!"

CHAPTER FOUR

GUESS WHO?

Brian was bored. He was sitting in the large reading room of the Gotham City Public Library. He counted the lights on the ceiling. He counted them again. He looked at a stain on the wall. He pretended it was a dragon. Then he pretended it was a dinosaur.

Brian was feeling lonely. And he was feeling scared. Suddenly he heard a crash.

He jumped to his feet. Maybe his mother had figured out his riddle and come to get him.

"Mom!" he called out. He rushed to the door. Then he stopped.

Instead of his mother, he saw a man. The man wore a mask and a green suit. The suit was covered in question marks.

"What's the tallest building in Gotham City?" asked the Riddler. "The library is the tallest building because it has so many stories!"

Brian stepped back. "Are you the Riddler?"

The Riddler grabbed Brian's arm. "Yes, I am," he said. "And now that I'm here, you're really being kidnapped."

Brian tried to pull away. But the Riddler held on tightly.

"They let me out of jail to help find you," the Riddler said. "But they'll want to put me back. You're going to help me stay out of jail!"

"Please," said Brian. "I want to go home!"

"You should have thought about that before you ran away," said the Riddler. "Why did you do it?"

"My mom says it's her job to follow clues and catch bad guys," said Brian. "She spends more time with them than she does with me. I wanted Mom to look for me instead of other people."

Still holding on to Brian, the Riddler wrote two notes. He put one on a reading table. He placed the other in a big book.

"Batman will catch you," Brian told the villain. "He's probably figuring out my riddle right now. He'll be here soon."

"I'm sure he will," said the Riddler. "That's why we have to hurry up — and leave!"

CHAPTER FIVE

FRIDAY BEFORE THURSDAY

Batman had indeed figured out Brian's riddle. He rushed to the library with Detective Fletcher and the commissioner. There Batman quickly found and read the Riddler's two notes.

"Meet me at the Gotham City Stadium," he told the detective and commissioner.

And then he was gone. How did he know Brian and the Riddler would be at the ballpark? Detective Fletcher read the first note. "Where does Friday come before Thursday?"

She spotted a dictionary on the table. Batman had left it there. Then she knew the answer to the riddle.

"Friday comes before Thursday in the dictionary!" she said.

Batman had left the dictionary open. A second note was taped under the word "Friday." The commissioner picked it up.

He read the note out loud. "Riddle me this. Your boy is worth more than gems to you. But is he worth more than the biggest diamond in Gotham City?"

"The biggest diamond in Gotham City,"

said Detective Fletcher. "Batman thinks
he means the baseball diamond at the
stadium!"

"Let's go!" said the commissioner.

CHAPTER SIX

BRIAN WAS STANDING AT *HOME PLATE.*

The ballpark was mostly dark. But lights shone on home plate. Brian was standing on the base.

Batman walked toward Brian.

"Stop!" Brian shouted. "The Riddler said something bad will happen if I step off the base."

Batman stopped.

"The Riddler also told me to tell you a riddle," Brian said. "Does it take longer to run from first base to second base or from second base to third base?"

Batman carefully walked toward

second base. He looked at the ground. "It takes longer from second to third base," he said, "because there's a 'shortstop' in the middle."

Batman walked between second and third base. He bent down and dug up the

dirt. He saw a red wire. Batman took a clipper from his utility belt and cut the wire. "Whatever booby trap the Riddler set won't work now!"

Just then, Detective Fletcher ran onto the field.

"Brian!" she cried.

Brian called back. "Mom!"

Batman nodded to Brian that it was now safe for him to leave the base. And Brian ran to his mother.

Commissioner Gordon joined them. "I guess we lost the Riddler," he said.

"He's at the lighthouse," Brian said.

"Did he tell you where he was going?" his mother asked.

"No," answered Brian. "But while he set the trap, he made me a bet. He bet that I couldn't guess which building in Gotham City weighed the least."

"Good work, Brian," said the commissioner.

"I'm on my way to the lighthouse," said Batman. "The Riddler will be back in jail by morning."

Before he left the stadium, Batman asked a riddle. "When things go wrong, what can you always count on?"

"Your family?" said Detective Fletcher.

"Batman?" said Brian Fletcher.

"Your fingers!" said Batman. Then off he went.

BATMAN *RACED OFF TO* THE LIGHTHOUSE.

And the next day, as Batman promised, the Riddler was back in jail—but for how long?

THE MAD HATTER

Written by **Brian Augustyn**
Illustrated by **Rick Burchett**

Batman created by Bob Kane

CHAPTER ONE

NOW YOU SEE IT, NOW YOU DON'T

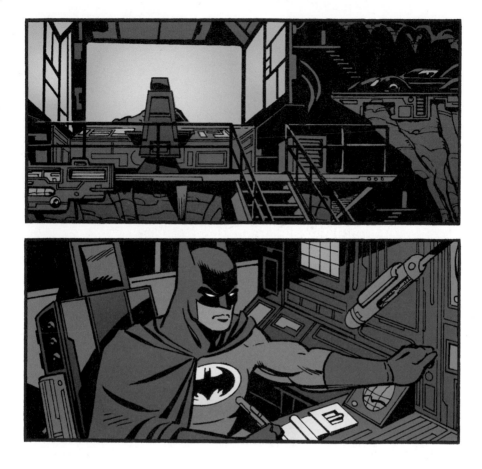

Bruce Wayne was one of the richest men in Gotham City. He lived in Wayne Manor, above a secret cave — the Batcave!

That's because Bruce was also Batman!

Every evening, Batman carefully checked his crime-fighting tools and equipment. Then he would go out on patrol.

"Ice cream! Get your ice cream here!"

It was sunny in Gotham City today. And Benny Diaz was feeling happy.

Benny sold ice cream from a cart. He pushed the cart through the streets of downtown Gotham City.

Benny loved being outdoors.

He loved selling sweet treats to people.

Benny loved his clean white uniform.

Most of all, he loved his peaked cap. It was almost like an army officer's hat.

"I am a general in the Ice Cream Army," Benny thought, and he smiled.

Benny pushed his cart past Gotham Square Park. There he saw something tall. It was covered with a big cloth.

Under the cloth was the new Gotham Unity Monument. Benny had read about it in the newspaper. The monument had names on it of cities from all over the world.

On Friday, Gotham City was going to show off the monument. A special top piece would be added then. It would be made of glass. It would hold treasures from all those great cities. Benny liked this idea. He smiled wider.

Then a pretty blond young girl waved to

him. She wore a blue dress and a white apron. Benny thought she looked like Alice from *Alice in Wonderland.*

"I'd like a green ice pop, please," the girl said sweetly.

Not many people liked green ice pops. Benny bent over the cold box of his cart and felt his hat slip off his head.

He stood up with the green pop. But the pretty girl was gone. And so was Benny's beautiful white cap.

Benny was sad and puzzled. Why would anyone take his hat?

That evening, people all over Gotham City wondered the same thing.

A garbage man's cap disappeared while he emptied trash cans.

A bicycle messenger lost his helmet at a stop sign.

A policewoman's cap disappeared while she directed traffic.

A sewer worker, a tour guide, and a sign painter had all lost their hats that day, too.

Someone was stealing hats!

The people of Gotham City wondered why anyone would do that. They didn't know that one of the city's worst bad guys had returned.

The Mad Hatter!

CHAPTER TWO

ART HISTORY

A CROWD GATHERED BEHIND THE WATCHMAN...

STRANGE—BUT I *LIKE* IT!

It was now nighttime. In the Museum of Fine Art, a watchman was on duty. He stopped to look at his favorite painting. It was by an artist named René Magritte.

The painting showed a man wearing a black suit and a black hat. A large, green apple floated in front of the man's face.

"Strange — but I like it!" the watchman said to himself.

Behind him, four people gathered silently. The blond girl who had taken Benny Diaz's hat was there.

Two very large men stood beside her. They looked like twin giants in matching striped sweaters.

The fourth person was the Mad Hatter. He had a bushy mustache and a tall top hat. His smile beamed brightly.

The Mad Hatter tapped the watchman on the shoulder. As the watchman turned from the painting, he saw the Mad Hatter standing behind him.

Before the watchman could say a word, the Mad Hatter pressed a button on his hat. A bright yellow smoke squirted from inside. The watchman breathed it in and fell asleep.

Out on the street, a dark, powerful car

drove silently by the museum. A man with
a mask was inside the car. It was Batman!
He spoke into a two-way radio.

"This is Batman. There's a break-in at the
Museum of Fine Art. Send the police!"

Batman had heard about the hat thefts. He knew that the Mad Hatter was back to make trouble. And Batman was sure that he would find the villain inside the museum... somewhere near the very famous and valuable painting with a hat!

Batman entered the museum with a key. The halls were dim. He moved quietly past statues and paintings. Soon Batman saw the Mad Hatter and his gang. They were stealing the painting of the man with the hat!

Batman pulled a small flashlight from his belt. He shone a bat-shaped light on the wall where the thieves worked. They jumped in surprise.

"It's Batman!" shouted the Mad Hatter. "Get him!"

BATMAN SHONE HIS BAT-LIGHT ON THE VILLAINS!

CHAPTER THREE

THE GREAT ESCAPE

The two big men moved to stop Batman.
Batman threw two capsules from his belt at
their feet. As the capsules broke, a shiny liquid
poured out.

It was oil, and the men slipped in it. They
fell down with a *BOOM!*

The Mad Hatter and the woman who
looked like Alice left the painting alone. They
ran to the center of the room. There they

stepped onto a large hat that lay on the floor.

Batman moved quickly. But the Mad Hatter's hat trick was even quicker. The hat lifted on large springs. The Mad Hatter and Alice bounced high into the air. They flew up and out a high window!

"Next time I won't be stopped!" the Mad Hatter shouted. "My next adventure will be my crowning glory!"

Batman watched them go. He knew he'd see them again.

The police took the two big men away. Outside the museum, Batman and Police Detective Renee Montoya spoke.

"These two are the Tweedle brothers, if you can believe it. Dee and Dominic," said Detective Montoya.

"Those names are perfect for the Mad

Hatter's Wonderland Gang," replied Batman. "He has an Alice, too."

Detective Montoya looked thoughtful. Something bothered her.

"Do you think the Mad Hatter stole all those different hats today just for practice?" she asked.

"Perhaps. The Mad Hatter likes stealing anything to do with hats," answered Batman. "Just like the painting tonight."

"Maybe it was his way of saying he was back," Montoya said with a smile.

"He's up to something. That's for sure. He said something about his 'crowning glory,'" said Batman.

He and the detective were silent. They were thinking.

"On Friday, the British Crown Jewels will

BATMAN KNEW THE MAD HATTER WAS UP TO SOMETHING.

be at Gotham Center," said the detective.

"And a crown is a kind of hat."

"That would attract the Mad Hatter all right," said Batman.

"The artist Magritte wanted people to see mysteries that are in plain sight. I think the Mad Hatter is telling us the same thing," he added. "We'll have to be ready for anything!"

CHAPTER FOUR

HAT TRICK

On Friday, Detective Montoya and many police officers were on guard at the Crown Jewels exhibit. Many people went to look at the fancy crowns. Gold and gems glittered in the bright lights.

There was no sign of the Mad Hatter and his gang. Still, the police waited. They were ready for anything.

At the same time, the Unity Monument was being unveiled across town.

Important people spoke. The crowd cheered. The large cloth was lifted off the monument.

"Gotham City dedicates this monument to world peace!" said Gotham's mayor. The crowd cheered louder.

A tall crane swung the top piece into place over the monument. Inside, the many treasures sparkled.

"This special capstone makes our wonderful monument even greater!" said the happy mayor.

Meanwhile, a man in an ice-cream vendor's uniform and cap pushed his cart through the crowd. He had a large and bushy mustache. He smiled as he looked up at the monument and its bright top.

Also in the crowd, a policewoman strolled by. She had long blond hair and looked a lot like Alice in Wonderland. She smiled, too.

A man in a sewer worker's hard hat climbed from a manhole. He moved toward the crane that held the capstone.

A bicycle messenger and a garbage man joined him. The three of them climbed into the crane's control cab.

"What the—" said the surprised crane

THE THREE MEN TIED UP THE CRANE OPERATOR.

operator. Before he could say more, the men tied him up.

Across the street, a sign painter in a beret looked up from his work and smiled. He had been sloppily painting a sign on a store door. Now he stopped.

The painter waved to a man driving a bus. The driver tipped his cap and drove forward. The big red bus bumped up onto the sidewalk and moved toward the monument.

The crowd cried out, "No! Watch out! Stop!" People began running when they saw the bus moving toward them. The ice-cream vendor hid his costume, tossed his white cap aside, and replaced it with a top hat. He was really the Mad Hatter! He chuckled nastily.

Then the Mad Hatter pulled a handful of hats from his cart. He tossed a flowered hat

toward the platform where the mayor stood
with other important people. He tossed a
baseball cap, too.

The hats squirted bright yellow smoke.
The people close to the smoke fell asleep.
Others ran away in fright.

"The treasure in the capstone is mine!"
shouted the Mad Hatter. "No one can stop me!"

CHAPTER FIVE

HAT ENOUGH?

THE *DARK KNIGHT* TOWERED OVER THE *MAD HATTER.*

A deep voice called out from above, "Why do criminals always say that?"

The Mad Hatter looked around. Who had spoken?

It was Batman!

"Take the capstone, men!" the Mad Hatter

shouted angrily. "Leave this bothersome bat to me!"

The Mad Hatter grabbed another of his knockout hats and got ready to throw it. At the same time, Batman swung down from a nearby building on his Batrope. He grabbed the large cloth that had covered the monument.

Batman tossed the cloth. It sailed down toward the Mad Hatter. It covered him like a blanket.

"Let me out!" the Mad Hatter shouted. He struggled, trapped underneath. But Batman moved on.

BATMAN SWUNG TOWARD THE MAD HATTER!

The Mad Hatter's men were lowering the monument's capstone onto the top of the bus. *THUMP!* Batman landed on the bus to stop them.

With a Batarang and his rope, Batman tied the men together. Then he left them dangling from the hook of the crane. "Help!" they shouted in fear. "Help!"

Back on the ground, the Mad Hatter finally came out from under the large cloth. His hat was crumpled. His hair and mustache were messy. And his suit was wrinkled and dirty.

The Mad Hatter knew his plan had failed! But he hoped he could still get away.

Suddenly, Batman was right next to him. Before the Mad Hatter could run, Batman grabbed the tall hat. He pulled down hard.

With the hat over his face, the Mad Hatter

BATMAN CAPTURED THE MAD HATTER WITH HIS OWN HAT!

couldn't see anything. There was no escape.
Batman watched as the police arrested
the villain.

"You were right, Batman," said Detective
Montoya. "He was after the capstone."

"There had to be a reason to steal so
many hats. If he was planning an indoor
crime, why take so many outdoor hats?"
Batman said. "And to the Mad Hatter, a
capstone is a kind of hat."

"Well, you saved the monument! And we
have the Mad Hatter and his gang," Detective
Montoya said with a smile.

"Not quite the entire gang...." said
Batman mysteriously.

CHAPTER SIX

PULLING THE WOOL OVER YOUR EYES

The girl who looked like Alice in Wonderland hurried away from Gotham Square.

Alice knew the Mad Hatter had been captured. She didn't want to be arrested, too! She was still dressed as a policewoman. So no one noticed her.

Suddenly, Alice's foot landed on something slippery. Her other foot skidded, too.

"Whoops!" Alice cried. She looked down as she fell. She had slipped on two green ice pops.

Nearby, Benny Diaz stood hatless and smiling. He was holding two ice-pop wrappers. Benny had recognized the girl who had stolen his hat. So he had come up with an idea. He had slid the pops under Alice's running feet so she would slip.

Seconds later, Batman arrived with the police. They thanked Benny for his help. And

BATMAN GAVE BENNY HIS HAT BACK...

...AND THEN SWUNG OFF WITH A SMILE!

the police took Alice away.

Batman smiled and offered something to Benny. It was Benny's white cap. The Mad Hatter had tossed it into the crowd. And Batman had found it.

Benny smiled as he put the cap back on. He was in uniform again. And it felt great.

Then Batman swung off with a smile.

Benny Diaz loved his job. He was sure that Batman loved his job, too.

THE PURR-FECT CRIME

Written by **Jason Hernandez-Rosenblatt**
Illustrated by **Rick Burchett**
Batman created by Bob Kane

CHAPTER ONE

ON THE PROWL

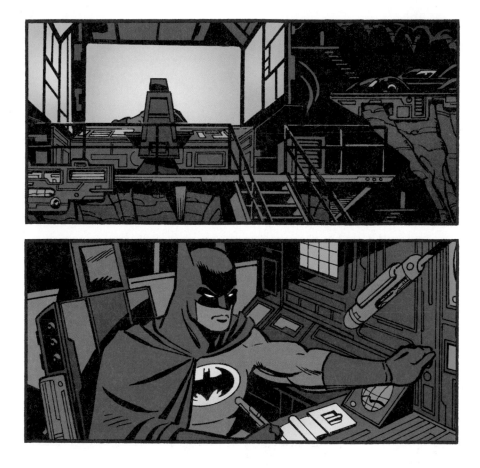

Bruce Wayne was one of the richest men in Gotham City. He lived in Wayne Manor, above a secret cave — the Batcave!

That's because Bruce was also Batman!

Every evening, Batman carefully checked his crime-fighting tools and equipment. Then he would go out on patrol.

On the roof of the Gotham Museum, Catwoman was so happy she could purr.

But she was as quiet as she could be. It was the middle of the night. Any noise could set off the alarms outside. And that would bring Batman!

IT WAS MIDNIGHT AT THE GOTHAM CITY MUSEUM...

Catwoman carefully cut a hole into the glass skylight with her glass cutter. The hole was just big enough for her to wiggle through.

She smiled as she dropped a rope through the hole. Quiet as a cat, she went down the rope into the dark museum.

The week before, she had stolen the plans for the museum's alarm system from the security company. So she knew just what she would find.

Four feet below her was a maze of hidden laser beams. If anything passed through any one of the beams, it would trigger the alarm.

So Catwoman pulled a small spray can from a bag on her belt. She sprayed the floor.

A cloud of smoke spread through the darkness. The beams of light shone bright red!

Catwoman dropped safely to the floor between the beams, like a cat who always lands on her feet.

Step one was done. It was time for step two.

Inside the glass display case in front of her were the very things she had come to the museum to steal—the Golden Cats of Bast!

CHAPTER TWO

A TAIL OF THREE CATS

Catwoman could not resist a valuable cat. And the twin statues of Bast, an ancient Egyptian goddess in the shape of a cat, were worth a lot of money. The statues, on loan from the Egyptian government, were solid gold, with glowing rubies for eyes and collars with big diamonds.

THE GOLDEN CATS OF BAST!

THE DISPLAY CASE AND THE ALARM WERE FROZEN SOLID!

But Catwoman knew there was an alarm
on the display case. And the slightest touch
to the case would set it off.

So she pulled out a second spray can.
She sprayed the thick glass with a special
freezing gas. A mist settled on the case.

Within seconds, the case and the alarm
were frozen solid!

Catwoman tapped the glass. The case
broke into pieces! With a happy purr,
Catwoman picked up the first statue.

Once, Catwoman had been a lonely little girl named Selina Kyle. And cats were her only friends.

Then she decided to become a super-villain. She chose the name Catwoman and dressed as a cat for her secret identity. Catwoman trusted cats, not people.

"Purr-fect!" said Catwoman as she put the first statue into her pouch. But as she reached for the second one, she heard a familiar voice.

"Sorry to spoil your night, Catwoman." And then the lights came on!

SUDDENLY, SHE HEARD A FAMILIAR VOICE!

CHAPTER THREE

NINE LIVES

"Batman!" she hissed. She whirled around.

"How did you know? I was so careful!"

The Caped Crusader stepped from the shadows into the light.

"I only had to wait for you," he said. "As soon as I heard about the Bast exhibit, I knew Catwoman wouldn't be able to resist trying to steal the statues."

"Try?" said Catwoman. "I've got one! And you can't catch me!"

Then Catwoman leaped for the rope that

BATMAN FOLLOWED AS SHE CLAWED HER WAY UP THE ROPE!

still hung from the skylight. Agile as a cat, she began to climb. But the Dark Knight was right behind her.

As Catwoman pulled herself through the hole in the skylight, she could see him climbing after her.

But he would never make it in time to stop her. As soon as she was on the roof, Catwoman untied the rope.

She watched with a smile as the rope fell down the hole. Batman landed with a *THUD!*

"We'll meet again soon, Catwoman!" shouted Batman.

CATWOMAN LET GO OF THE ROPE.

Catwoman didn't want to leave behind the second statue. But she had no choice.

"Batman is always one step ahead of me," she thought as she leaped across the rooftops. "How does he always know where I am?"

Then she remembered something. Batman expected *Catwoman* to steal the statues.

"What if I were *not* Catwoman?" she thought as she escaped into the night.

CHAPTER FOUR

CAT GOT YOUR TONGUE?

Batman sat at the master control center in the Batcave. He looked at the giant computer monitor.

Alfred, his butler and lifelong friend, stepped out of the elevator carrying a tray.

"Here you are, sir," Alfred said. He put the tray down next to Batman. "I trust the night went well?"

"Not at all," Batman said. "Catwoman escaped with one of the statues."

"She is rather a sneaky one," Alfred said.

"Yes, she is," said Batman. "But I can usually guess where she'll strike next."

"She'll try to steal the second statue, of course," said Alfred.

"She'll try," said Batman. "She'll certainly try!"

CHAPTER FIVE

HERE, KITTY, KITTY!

Two days later, Batman was at the Egyptian Embassy in Gotham City where the second Bast statue was being returned for safekeeping. In a little while, an armored car would pull up in front of the building. Police officers would carry a safe with the statue inside it into the embassy.

Batman knew Catwoman would try to steal the statue. But he was ready for her.

He made sure this event was on the news. And he hid inside the guardhouse on a busy street.

Exactly on time, the armored car drove up to the embassy surrounded by four police cars.

Through a crack in the guardhouse door, Batman saw the cars stop in front of the embassy.

BATMAN WAS READY FOR CATWOMAN.

BATMAN WATCHED FROM HIS HIDING PLACE.

He watched as the Egyptian Ambassador came out of the embassy to meet the armored car.

A policeman and a policewoman pulled the special safe out of the car.

Then, following the ambassador, the police officers hurried inside the embassy, carrying the safe.

There was no sign of Catwoman anywhere!

"Where could she be?" Batman thought. "She could never resist a good cat crime!"

Batman was trying to understand his mistake when the armored car drove away, followed by three police cars.

He was about to leave the guardhouse when he saw the policewoman run out of the embassy alone. She hopped into the fourth police car and sped away.

"Didn't the policewoman go into the

embassy with her partner and the ambassador?" Batman wondered. "Where are they?"

He rushed into the embassy and found both men on the floor. The open safe lay between them. It was empty!

Then Batman smelled knockout gas. "Catwoman!" he said.

BATMAN SMELLED KNOCKOUT GAS!

CHAPTER SIX

CAT'S OUT OF THE BAG

CATWOMAN HAD OUTSMARTED BATMAN!

Catwoman purred as she drove away from the embassy. The second gold statue sat on the seat next to her.

She couldn't remember the last time she had been this happy. She had outsmarted Batman! And now both statues were hers!

But how had she done it?

Catwoman had realized she had to steal the statue not as Catwoman but as plain old Selina Kyle.

That morning, she had put on a policewoman's uniform over her costume.

She had taken the place of the policewoman who was supposed to help carry the statue. Then she had walked right past Batman.

Catwoman knew Batman must have been near the embassy, watching. But she also knew he had been looking for Catwoman, not Selina Kyle.

Catwoman purred again as she drove through Gotham's streets. Suddenly, the car radio crackled on.

"This is Batman! A police car has been stolen. It was last seen headed east on Sprang Avenue!"

But Catwoman wasn't worried. She knew Batman would figure out what had happened. She had planned for that.

She made several turns through the busy city streets. She made sure no one was following her.

Then she drove into a deserted alley.

SHE HAD A PLAN!

There, the feline felon threw away the stolen policewoman's uniform. She was Catwoman once again.

Then, clutching the statue, she climbed a fire escape and ran across the rooftops toward home.

CATWOMAN...

...LEAPED ACROSS ROOFTOPS TOWARD HOME.